Original
Fairy Tales
from the Brothers Grimm

Original
Fairy Tales
from the Brothers Grimm

CLASSIC EDITION

Illustrated by Anastassija Archipowa

Retold by Jane Resnick

DERRYDALE BOOKS

TORMONT

Copyright © Verlag J.F. Schreiber GmbH,
"Esslinger in OBV",
Postfach 285, 7300 Esslingen/West Germany
English text © 1991 Joshua Morris Publishing, Inc.
221 Danbury Road, Wilton, Connecticut 06897
All rights reserved.
This 1992 edition published by
Tormont Publications Inc.
338 Saint Antoine St. East
Montreal, Canada H2Y 1A3
Tel. (514) 954-1441
Fax (514) 954-1443
Printed in Hong Kong
ISBN 2-89429-061-6

Table of Contents

Cinderella

Cinderella

There was once a rich man who lived with his wife and daughter in a great house. His wife became very ill and when she knew she was going to die, she left her young daughter with these tender words:

"Do not be sad, my dear child, for I will always watch over you, and the birds of the forest will protect you."

But the girl cried bitterly. And even after a year, she visited her mother's grave faithfully. While she was there, the birds of the forest comforted her.

She became even sadder when her father married a cold, greedy woman with two daughters who laughed at their stepsister for her gentleness and love for the birds. They wanted her father's wealth and were jealous of her beauty.

Because the father was often away and unaware of his household, the stepmother and stepsisters told him that his daughter had become stubborn and bad, and asked to punish her. At first he did not believe them, but his daughter never defended herself. So from that day on, she was given an old, ugly dress to wear, and she was treated like the lowest of servants.

Her sisters teased her by throwing peas and lentils into the ashes and making her pick them out. In this way, she became covered with cinders— and they called her Cinderella.

Alone and sad, Cinderella had only the birds of the forest to comfort her when she visited her mother's grave each day.

One day, when the father left for a long journey, he asked the stepsisters what gift they would

like upon his return.

"A dress of silk, jewels and pearls," they demanded.

"Cinderella?" he asked sadly, for he thought she was as awful as he had been told.

"I would like a branch if one brushes against you," she said.

Her sisters laughed at this.

"Stupid girl!" the older said as soon as the father left. Then she

threw a handful of lentils into the ashes.

"Sort these!" she ordered. "Save the clean ones for soup."

Cinderella fell to her knees and began sorting the lentils.

When the father returned, the two sisters showed off their new finery, but Cinderella took the hazel twig her father brought her and planted it by her mother's grave. In time, it grew into a fine tree, loved by all the birds of the forest.

One day Cinderella scraped her knee on the hearth. When

she went to her mother's grave she wept and said: *Hear my wish, my hazel tree: I need some comfort for my knee.*

A silver bird flew down from the branches. With its own feather, the bird brushed the soot from Cinderella's knee.

When Cinderella got back to the house, she found her stepsisters in a frantic rush.

"Bring me my ribbons! Where are my pearls?" they cried.

"The King has invited the daughters of the house to a ball," the stepmother said. "It will last three nights and the prince will choose a bride."

"Why am I not to go?" Cinderella asked.

"You!" cried the stepmother. "You are too ugly and dirty!"

But the father, while he was preparing to leave for yet another journey, overheard her.

"She *is* my daughter," he said.

"If she can finish her work, she can go," she replied.

But as soon as the father left, the stepmother threw a huge handful of lentils into the ashes.

"If you sort these and bring me a bowl of good ones in an hour, you may go," she said.

Cinderella ran to her mother's grave and said: *Hear my wish, my hazel tree: I need my birds to work for me.*

The little silver bird and all the other forest birds flew to the kitchen. They began picking the lentils from the ashes with their beaks and dropping the good ones into a bowl.

Before the hour, the task was complete and Cinderella took the bowl to her stepmother.

"I have finished," she said in a voice filled with hope.

The stepmother was startled and did not know what to do. She was determined to keep Cinderella from going to the ball, for she knew she was far lovelier than her own daughters.

"You still cannot go," she said. "You are filthy and have no clothes for a ball."

Cinderella wept and wept. Her stepmother became so annoyed that she marched into the kitchen, filled a huge bowl with lentils and threw them all into the ashes.

"You may go if you pick these out in an hour," she said. She was sure Cinderella could not.

So Cinderella ran to her mother's grave again and said: *Hear my wish, my hazel tree: I need my birds to work for me.*

And the silver bird flew down again and within an hour all the lentils were sorted. But this time, her stepmother was very angry and said:

"Go away! I do not believe you did what I ordered. You may not come with us!"

Then she and the stepsisters hurried into the coach that took them to the ball.

Weeping, Cinderella went to her mother's grave once more.

After the silver bird comforted her with his singing, she said: *Hear my wish, my hazel tree: I need a dress to cover me.*

At this, the bird flew down with a magnificent gold and silver dress with beautiful dancing slippers. Cinderella thanked the bird. She bathed and dressed and went to the ball.

There, everyone stared at her, for she was, by far, the most beautiful girl in the room. Even her own stepsisters and stepmother admired her without realizing who she was.

As soon as Cinderella entered the ballroom, the prince asked her to dance. From that moment

he would dance with no one else. Beautiful Cinderella danced in a dream of happiness.

But as the hour grew late, Cinderella knew she must go home, for she was afraid she would be punished if her family had known she had been to the ball.

"I will take you home," said the prince eagerly, but she fled down the stairs so fast that he could not catch her.

Cinderella was in her old dress by the hearth when her step-mother and stepsisters returned. They never suspected that she was the beautiful maiden who stole the prince's heart.

On the second evening of the

ball, her father was still away, so as soon as her stepsisters and stepmother drove off in the coach, Cinderella ran to her mother's grave and said: *Hear my wish, my hazel tree: I need a dress to cover me.*

The bird brought her another dress even more beautiful than the first one, more intricately embroidered and with more gold than silver. The dancing slippers were like the wings of delicate, brightly colored butterflies.

At the ball, once again, everyone marveled at Cinderella's beauty, the prince most of all. He had eyes only for Cinderella and would dance with no one else. The music seemed to be just for the two of them.

"Please let me take you

home," the prince said to his mysterious dancing partner. "I want to know where you live and who your father is."

But when the hour was late, Cinderella escaped, and even though the prince followed closely, she ran swiftly into the woods and climbed a tree. She hid in the tree until he gave up the search.

When her stepsisters arrived home, they found her asleep as before and thought she could not hear their grumbling about the beautiful girl who captured the prince's attention.

"Never mind," they said to one another. "Perhaps she will not be at the ball tomorrow. Or perhaps the prince will notice one of us instead."

On the third night of the ball, Cinderella again waited for her stepmother and stepsisters to leave. She ran to her mother's grave where she said: *Hear my wish, my hazel tree: I need a dress to cover me.*

The bird brought her a magnificent dress that glowed like shimmering sunbeams and slippers that sparkled like dazzling crystal. That night the prince vowed that he would not lose her. During the ball, his servants covered the stairs with sticky pine tar.

When Cinderella felt she must leave, she slipped from his embrace and fled. But this time, the stairs prevented her from running so quickly. One of her slippers stuck in the tar and she had to leave it behind on the stair or be caught.

The next morning the prince took the slipper to his father, the king, and said:

"My bride will be the maiden whose foot fits this slipper. She is the beautiful princess I have danced with every night."

The prince set out that day

and traveled to the house of every person invited to the ball. Girls all over the kingdom pretended to have lost a slipper, for they were anxious to be queen. But the slipper was too small for everyone who tried it on.

Cinderella's house was the last place the prince came to.

"Surely, I will find my princess here," he thought.

The father was still not at home, so the stepmother took her older daughter into her room to try the slipper on.

"It is too small," the girl said. "Four toes will fit but the fifth will not squeeze in."

"Just bend the toe under," the determined mother said.

"I can hardly walk!" gasped the girl.

But her mother led her daughter out to the prince.

"Come with me," he said graciously, "for the shoe is indeed on your foot."

The girl managed to walk to the carriage without limping, but the prince felt in his heart that something was not right.

As the prince's coach passed Cinderella's mother's grave, the birds of the forest flew around his coach. The silver bird whispered in the prince's ear: *Good prince, you know not what you do. Her foot is bent inside the shoe!*

So the prince asked the step-sister to get down from the coach and walk with him under the trees. But the girl's toes were so cramped she could barely move.

"You are not my true bride," he said angrily, and returned her to her parents' house.

"It must be my other daughter whom you want," the stepmother said. She forced her other child to squeeze her foot into the slipper.

Once again the prince was fooled until the little silver bird whispered to him: *Good prince, you know not what you do. Her foot is bent inside that shoe!*

And as he was bringing the girl back to her door, the father returned home.

"Is there no other girl here?" the prince asked.

"None but my two," the stepmother replied.

"But there's Cinderella," the father said.

"She's just a servant girl," the stepmother replied sharply.

At last, Cinderella's father grew angry and said, "She's *my* daughter and she *will* be given a chance!" And he sent for her.

The dazzling slipper slid easily onto Cinderella's slender foot, and this time the prince knew in his heart that he had found the maiden he was looking for. So he led her gently to his coach and took her away with him.

As they passed the hazel tree, the silver bird sang:

Good prince, you've found your bride so true: See how her foot fits in the shoe!

Soon the king held another ball—in honor of the wedding of the prince and Cinderella.

Little
Red Riding Hood

Little Red Riding Hood

Once upon a time there was a girl called Little Red Riding Hood because she always wore a colorful red hat. She was a sweet, kind child and everyone liked her, especially her dear grandmother who loved her most of all.

One day, Red Riding Hood's mother said, "Take this food to Grandmother. She is ill. Seeing you will make her feel better.

But go straight through the woods," her mother added. "Do not stop to talk to anyone."

Little Red Riding Hood's grandmother lived on the other side of the forest from the village. It was a sunny day, and Little Red Riding Hood was enjoying the long walk. She forgot all about strangers.

Suddenly, a wolf approached and spoke to her in a gentle voice that hid his wickedness.

"Good morning," said the wolf. "Where are you going?"

"To my grandmother's house," the girl replied.

The sly wolf smiled, trying to hide his big teeth. He was thinking that Little Red Riding Hood would make a tender meal. And if he was clever, he could have the grandmother too.

"Where does she live?" the wolf asked kindly.

Little Red Riding Hood described the spot on the edge of the wood where her grandmother's cottage stood beneath three oak trees.

Then the wolf said sweetly, "Look at all these beautiful flowers! I am sure your grandmother would enjoy having some for her table."

Little Red Riding Hood glanced at all the wildflowers and began to pick them.

"I must be off!" said the wolf.

So while Little Red Riding Hood picked a bouquet of wildflowers, the cunning wolf rushed through the forest to Grandmother's cottage. He found it easily under the three oak trees. Licking his lips, he knocked on the door.

"Who is there?" called the old woman from her bed.

"It's Little Red Riding Hood

bringing you a basket of food," said the hungry wolf, disguising his voice.

"Come in," said Grandmother cheerfully. And she climbed out of bed to open the door.

No sooner was the wolf inside than he gobbled up the poor old lady. Then he quickly wrapped himself in her shawl, put on her pink nightcap, jumped into her bed and pulled the covers up to his face.

He did not have very long to wait. Soon Little Red Riding Hood arrived with her arms filled with wildflowers.

"Good morning, Grandmother," she called, coming in the open door.

Little Red Riding Hood was worried when she did not hear her grandmother reply. She went up to the bed and peered closely at her grandmother. She thought she looked very strange.

"Come closer and give me a kiss, child," the wolf said.

"But Grandmother, what big ears you have!" she exclaimed.

"The better to hear you with," said the crafty wolf.

"And what big eyes you have!" cried the child.

"The better to see you with, my dear Red Riding Hood," answered the wolf.

"And, Grandmother, what big teeth you have!" said Little Red Riding Hood.

"The better to *eat* you with!" cried the wolf. And he sprang out of bed and swallowed poor Little Red Riding Hood.

The greedy wolf was so full and tired with Grandmother and Little Red Riding Hood in his stomach. He climbed back into bed and fell asleep, snoring loudly.

Now a hunter who was passing by the old woman's cottage saw the open door and heard the deep, loud snoring.

"I must see if anything is wrong," he thought.

When he saw the wolf asleep, he angrily raised his gun to shoot. But at that moment it occurred to him that the wolf

might have eaten the old woman.

"Perhaps I can still save her!" he thought.

So quickly, he slit open the sleeping wolf. And much to his surprise, Little Red Riding Hood *and* her grandmother emerged from the wolf's stomach frightened, but unharmed.

Once they realized they were safe, they turned to the hunter and thanked him.

Then Grandmother hugged and kissed Little Red Riding Hood. Little Red Riding Hood gave her grandmother the wildflowers she had picked and food she had brought. She was relieved and happy to see her grandmother well.

And Little Red Riding Hood knew then that she would never again talk to strangers in the forest and *never* stop on the way to Grandmother's house.

Sleeping Beauty

Sleeping Beauty

Once there lived a King and Queen who longed for a child, but they had none. At last, the Queen gave birth to a baby girl. She was so charming that the King could not contain his joy.

He decided to hold a great celebration and invite all the Wise Women of the kingdom — all except one, for there were thirteen Wise Women and only twelve golden plates. At the end of the feast, each one gave a magic gift to the tiny Princess. One gave the Princess beauty, another, virtue, a third, wisdom.

But before the last had spoken, the Wise Woman who had not been invited burst into the room. Furious at being neglected, she brought a curse instead of a blessing.

Bitterly, she called out, "When the Princess is fifteen, she will prick her finger on a spindle and die!" She stormed out without uttering another word.

But then the twelfth Wise Woman stepped forward, for she

had not yet given her gift.

"I cannot lift the curse," she said, "but I can alter it. The Princess will not die. She will fall into a deep sleep, which will last one hundred years. Then she will be awakened by a King's son."

Grief-stricken, the King vowed to protect his child. He ordered that every spindle in the kingdom be destroyed.

As time passed, all the Wise Women's blessings were fulfilled. The Princess grew to be beautiful, kind, sweet-natured and wise, and all who knew her loved her.

On her fifteenth birthday, it so happened that the inquisitive princess was wandering through the great castle exploring. High in a tower, she discovered a strange room, where there sat an old woman busily spinning wool. The Princess, who had never seen this before, was very curious.

"What are you doing?" she asked.

"Spinning," said the woman.

"May I try?" asked the girl.

Yet as soon as she took the spindle into her hand, she pricked her finger, and the wicked curse came true. The Princess fell upon a bed in the

room and a deep sleep came over her. Suddenly, everyone else in the castle fell asleep, too.

The King and Queen fell asleep on their thrones and the people of their court fell asleep wherever they were. The horses went to sleep in the stables, the dogs in the yard, the pigeons on the roof, and the flies on the wall. Even the fire in the hearth flickered and then stopped burning. The meat that was roasting went cold.

And the cook, who was about to pull the kitchen boy's hair because he had done something wrong, let him go and fell asleep with a great snore. The kitchen boy fell asleep, too. The breeze stopped blowing, and not a leaf stirred in the trees in front of the palace. Everything in the castle was silent.

All around the castle a thorny briar hedge began to grow where there had once been fields of beautiful flowers. Every year the hedge grew higher and thicker until it surrounded and hid the palace, so that nothing could be seen, not even the flag that flew from the roof of the highest tower, now standing still.

But the castle and its inhabitants were not forgotten. The story of the beautiful sleeping Princess was told far and wide and became a legend throughout the land. Over the years, many princes came and tried to force their way through the briar bushes to the palace. But none succeeded. They were cut by the thorns of the briar bushes and forced to turn away.

After many, many years a Prince came to the country

and heard an old man tell the story of the castle behind the briar hedge. He described the beautiful Princess who lay sleeping there with the King and Queen and all their court. The old man also knew from his father that many princes had tried to force themselves through the fierce briar hedge, only to fail.

But the young Prince said, "I am not afraid. I must see the lovely sleeping Princess."

The old man tried to dissuade him, but the Prince would not listen.

Now it so happened that the hundred years had passed and the day had come for the Princess to awaken. When the Prince approached the briar hedge, the briars blossomed into flowers. A path through the hedge opened for him, and he passed through unharmed.

In the courtyard he saw the horses and dogs lying asleep. On the roof the pigeons were curled up with their heads beneath their wings.

When he entered the castle it seemed haunted with a ghostly silence. The people of the court

were asleep in the great hall, and the King and Queen were asleep on their thrones. The Prince searched the palace. At last he came to the tower where the Princess lay sleeping. She was so beautiful that he bent down and gently kissed her. At the touch of his lips, the Princess opened her eyes and smiled sweetly.

Then they went down from the tower together. As they descended, the King and Queen and the whole court woke up and looked at each other in wonder. The horses and dogs and pigeons and flies came to life. The fire began crackling, and the meat resumed roasting. The cook pulled the kitchen boy's hair, and all returned to normal.

Then the wedding of the Prince and the Princess was celebrated in splendor. They lived happily in the castle until the end of their days.

Snow White
and the Seven Dwarfs

Snow White
and the Seven Dwarfs

On a snowy winter day, a beautiful queen sat at her window sewing. Her splendid palace had walls of fine marble and windows of smooth, black ebony. Suddenly she pricked her finger with the needle, and a few drops of blood fell outside the window.

The queen gazed at the bright red pattern they made by the window on the pure white snow.

"I wish I had a daughter," she said, "with skin as white as snow, lips as red as blood, and hair as black as ebony."

Soon the queen did give birth

The king was sad but also very lonely, and so he married again. The new queen was beautiful but very cruel. Although she was not a witch, she knew evil magic. She was so vain that she could not stand the thought of another woman more beautiful than she. The new queen used her evil magic to create a mirror that would always tell her who was the fairest in the land. Every morning the queen stood before her magic mirror and said: *Mirror, mirror upon my wall, Who is the fairest one of all?* The mirror always answered: *You are the fairest of all.*

At that, the Queen always smiled and was satisfied.

But as little Snow White grew, she became more lovely every day. One day, when the girl was quite grown, the queen looked into her mirror and said: *Mirror, mirror upon my wall, Who is the fairest one of all?*

to a baby girl, but sadly, she lived only long enough to see that her wish came true. The child did have skin as white as snow, lips as red as blood, and hair as black as ebony. Before she died the queen named the beautiful baby Snow White.

The mirror answered: *Queen, you once were the fairest in this place. But little Snow White is fairer of face.*

The Queen flew into a rage and could not contain her jealousy. She could not bear the sight of Snow White and became sick with envy. At last she called a hunter and ordered him to bring the girl into the forest and kill her.

"Bring me back her liver as proof that you have killed her," the cruel Queen demanded.

The hunter was afraid to refuse. Reluctantly, he took Snow White into the forest, but when he drew his knife, she cried out, "Please spare me! I will run deep

into the woods, and the queen will never see my face again! Spare my life!"

The hunter put his knife down and let Snow White go. On his way home, he killed a wild boar and brought its liver to the heartless queen who ate it.

"Now I can have peace at last," the haughty queen said with satisfaction.

Meanwhile, poor Snow White, alone in the forest, was terribly frightened. She did not know how to find food or a place to sleep. She could think of nothing but to run — through thickets and brambles, over sharp stones and streams. The terrified girl saw shadows behind every tree, but the wild beasts took pity on the beautiful girl and did not harm her. Snow White stopped to rest and sometimes weep, but each time, she was afraid that she was not far enough from the dreadful queen.

So she kept running deeper and deeper into the forest. At last, when she felt so tired that her legs would not carry her another step, she came upon a little tiny cottage. It was so small that it looked as if it might have been built for a child.

Snow White knocked, but no one answered. It seemed that no one was at home so she gently pushed open the door. Then Snow White stepped inside.

Here was a home for a child indeed. Or for several children! Everything was child-sized, and there were *seven* of everything. Around the fireplace were seven small, cozy chairs and seven pairs of slippers. On a pipe rack, were seven little pipes. There were seven hooks by the door for coats and seven pairs of boots.

Snow White gazed around the cottage in astonishment. She felt like a giant here where everything was so small.

Her eyes came to rest on a table in the corner. Seven little chairs of all different shapes were pulled up to the table. Seven places had been set, each with a cup and plate, and a fork, knife, and spoon.

It looked like a meal had been prepared. On the plates were stew and potatoes, and in the cups was wine. Snow White was so hungry that she took a little from each place. This was because she did not want to take anyone's entire meal.

Then she found the bedroom where there were seven little beds. She tried each of them, for she was very tired. None were quite right except the last one, where she lay down and soon fell fast asleep.

At dark, the owners of the house returned. They were seven dwarfs who went off to the mountains every day to mine for

gold. As soon as they lit their candles, they knew that someone had been there.

"Someone has been sitting in my chair!" said the first dwarf.

"And using my fork," said the second dwarf.

"And my cup!" said the third.

"And my spoon!" cried the fourth dwarf.

"And eating my stew!" said the fifth.

"My potatoes!" said the sixth.

"And someone is in the bedroom!" exclaimed the seventh, seeing the open door.

They all rushed into the room. Each dwarf noticed that his bed was slightly messed. But the seventh found Snow White asleep in his bed and called all the others. They crowded around and stared at the sleeping Snow White.

"What a beautiful girl," they said. "She must have been lost in the forest. Poor child."

And so they let her sleep.

In the morning, Snow White woke up to find all the dwarfs around her, and she cried out in fright. But they were very kind dwarfs. They asked her name and how she had come to their house. When they heard about the wicked queen, they felt sorry for her and politely asked her to stay with them.

"Thank you," Snow White said, "for I cannot go home. But what can I do in return?"

"There *is* something," said the first dwarf. "We really could use help cooking and cleaning."

Snow White laughed in delight. "I will gladly cook and clean for you," she said.

So every morning the dwarfs went off to the mine, and Snow White cooked and cleaned. The dwarfs warned her never, *never* to let anyone in the house. "The wicked queen will soon find out that you are alive," they said.

The dwarfs were right. Soon the jealous queen went to her mirror and said: *Mirror, mirror upon my wall, Who is the fairest one of all?*

And the mirror answered: *O Queen, you are the fairest of all in this place, but little Snow White, living in the forest with seven little men, is still the one fairer of face.*

The queen was so angry she would have killed the hunter had he not fled the kingdom.

"I must have Snow White's life!" she raged. And the queen thought of an awful plan. She painted her face as an old woman and dressed in rags. Then, taking a basket, she made her way to the seven dwarfs' cottage in the woods. She knocked on the door and said, "Laces and sashes for sale; Ribbons in colors so pale."

Snow White came to the window and called, "What are you selling, old woman?"

"I sell many things," said the wicked queen. "Aren't these sashes beautiful?"

Snow White was enchanted by the colorful sashes. What harm could there be in this old woman, she thought. So she opened the door and let the woman in.

The queen slipped a sash around Snow White's waist and pulled it so tight that Snow White could not catch her breath. She fell down as if dead.

"Who is the fairest now!" cried the evil queen as she left.

When the dwarfs returned, they found their beloved Snow White on the cottage floor. They tried everything to revive her. At last, they noticed the new sash around her waist and quickly re-moved it. Slowly, Snow White began to breathe and told them about the peddler woman.

"That was the wicked queen!" they cried. And they begged her never, *never* to let anyone in

again. Snow White promised she would not.

That same night the queen went to her mirror and said: *Mirror, mirror upon my wall, Who is the fairest one of all?*

And the mirror answered: *O Queen, you are the fairest of all in this place, but Little Snow White, living in the forest with seven little men, is still the fairer of face.*

The queen was furious. "I shall make a beautiful poison comb," she said. "No girl will be able to resist it."

The cruel queen came to Snow White's window disguised as a poor woman.

"Please buy this comb," she pleaded. "It is all I have left for money to feed my children."

Snow White felt sorry for the poor woman.

"I am not supposed to let any-one in," she said, "but you may stay a moment."

And so she let the woman in. Then the wicked queen put

the poison comb in Snow White's hair, and the girl fell to the ground as if she were dead.

Imagine how the dwarfs felt when they saw Snow White lying on the floor again! They could not awaken her until the oldest one saw the comb and removed it. Breathing at last, she told them what happened.

"You must not go near *any* stranger," they warned her.

And so Snow White promised that she would not.

But the next day the queen went to her mirror and said: *Mirror, mirror upon my wall, Who is the fairest one of all?*

And the mirror answered: *O Queen, you are the fairest of all in the place, but little Snow White, living in the forest with seven little men, is still the one fairer of face.*

The queen set out to destroy Snow White immediately. She created a beautiful poison apple, but put the poison on only one side. Then she rushed to the cottage disguised as a farmer's wife.

This time when she knocked at the door, Snow White answered, "Go away, I am not allowed to talk to strangers."

"No matter" said the wicked queen. "I have an apple to sell, but I will eat it myself."

Snow White was curious and came to the window. The woman was eating the most delicious looking apple. The girl looked at it longingly.

"I will give you half," said the woman to Snow White.

Seeing that the woman had already bitten into it, Snow White thought it could do no harm. So when the evil queen gave her the poisoned half, she took it gratefully. As soon as she took a bite, Snow White fell down once more, but this time she was cold as ice.

"Nothing can save you now!" cried the queen. And she raced home and she asked her mirror: *Mirror, mirror upon my wall, Who is the fairest one of all?* The mirror answered: *You are the fairest of all.* And at last the queen was happy.

That night when the dwarfs came home, they found Snow White lying on the floor, but they could not revive her. They wept and wept and finally set about to build her a coffin.

Somehow, Snow White looked as beautiful as when she was alive. They could not bear to bury her in the dark ground, so they built her a coffin of glass. They placed it in a grove and guarded it day and night.

Years went by, but Snow White did not awaken. Snow White never changed except to grow into a beautiful woman. One day a prince rode by and seeing Snow White, he was overcome with pity and love.

"I will give you all the gold I have for this coffin," he said.

But the dwarfs said, "We would not part with her for all the riches in the world."

"Then give it freely to me," said the prince, "for I cannot live without her."

The dwarfs were moved by his love and could not refuse.

The prince ordered his servants to take the coffin and carry it away. As they did, one servant stumbled on a root. Snow White was jolted, and the piece of poison apple that was stuck in her throat came free — she had not swallowed it after all!

Snow White opened her eyes and sat up, completely alive.

"Where am I?" she asked, lifting the lid of the coffin.

"With me!" cried the prince.

"And with us!" said the dwarfs, dancing with joy.

The prince told Snow White how he loved her and begged her to marry him.

"I will," she said, "as long as the dwarfs may visit me."

Everyone happily agreed. The prince departed, looking forward to the wonderful wedding celebration to come.

Now one of the guests at the prince's wedding was Snow White's stepmother, but she did not know who the bride would be. Dressed for the wedding, she went to her mirror and asked: *Mirror, mirror upon my wall, Who is the fairest one of all?*

And the mirror answered: *Queen, you are the fairest of all in this place. But Queen Snow White is fairer of face.*

The queen was so furious she hurled the mirror across the room. One of the pieces hit the wall and flew back at her, piercing her heart. She fell down dead, never to harm Snow White again.

Puss in Boots

Puss in Boots

Once there was a miller. When he died, his belongings were divided among his three sons. The oldest son took the mill. The middle son got the donkey. And the youngest son was left with the cat named Puss.

"How can I survive with just this cat?" the young man grumbled sadly.

Now Puss was a clever cat and eager to please his new master.

"Don't be down-hearted," Puss said. "Get me a pair of

hunting boots and a sack. I'll prove how useful I can be."

The miller's son figured that a cat that could talk must be very smart indeed. So he got Puss a sack with a strong cord and a pair of leather boots.

Puss put on his boots, threw the sack over his shoulder and headed for a glen where there were plenty of rabbits. He put a carrot and some lettuce in the sack, then hid behind a tree.

Soon a foolish rabbit hopped into the bag to eat the lettuce. Quickly, Puss yanked the cord.

Taking his catch, Puss marched to the king's castle.

"Your majesty," he said, "this rabbit is a gift from my master, the Marquis of Carabas."

"I have never heard of the Marquis of Carabas," the king replied. "But tell him that I am pleased to accept his gift."

The next day Puss went to a wheat field, filled the sack with grain and caught two partridges. Again he went to the king.

"The Marquis of Carabas wishes you to enjoy these fine

birds at your dinner table," Puss said with a bow. Again the king gladly accepted.

On the third day, Puss snared two lovely trout and presented them to the king.

"The Marquis of Carabas must be a fine and generous gentleman," the king said. "I send him my heartfelt gratitude."

While in the court, Puss learned that the king would be riding by the riverbank in a part of the country he had never seen. His daughter, the most beautiful princess in the world, would accompany him.

Puss ran to the miller's son and said, "If you do exactly as I say, your fortune will be made. Tomorrow, go and bathe in the river, but remember, your new name is the Marquis of Carabas. Leave the rest to me!"

The young man was puzzled but did as he was told.

The next day, after the miller's son jumped in the river and swam off shore, Puss hid his master's ragged clothes behind a large rock.

Then, as the coach carrying the king and princess came down the road, Puss cried out, "Help!

Help! My master, the Marquis of Carabas, is drowning!"

The king recognized the cat who had brought him so many gifts and stopped the carriage.

"Save that man!" he shouted and ordered his guards to rescue the drowning "Marquis."

ing as grand as any marquis. Puss introduced him to the king.

"My dear Marquis," said the king, "I am so pleased to make your acquaintance. Let me present my daughter."

The princess cast a tender glance at the young man. Her heart was filled with love for this handsome miller's son.

"Please ride with us," the king said. The surprised young man sat next to the princess, enjoying her loving gaze.

Puss, happy that his plan was working, ran ahead. Soon he came to a field where peasants were mowing hay.

"The king is coming!" he shouted. "You must tell him that these fields belong to the Marquis of Carabas. If you do not, you will be chopped into mincemeat!"

The peasants were terrified. So when the king approached and asked, "To whom do these fields belong?" they answered,

Puss thanked him fervently and explained to the king that miserable thieves had stolen his master's clothes.

Immediately, the king sent his men for a fine suit for the "Marquis of Carabas." The miller's son emerged in his new clothes look-

"To the Marquis of Carabas!"

The king was very impressed and turned to the Marquis and said, "Your field is rich with a fine and abundant crop."

The young man smiled graciously but said nothing.

Meanwhile Puss ran ahead until he came to a wheat field where the workers were busy with the harvest.

"The king is coming!" he shouted. "You must tell him that these fields belong to the Marquis of Carabas. If you do not, you will be chopped into mincemeat!"

Again the frightened workers did as they were told. And Puss raced ahead threatening every-

one until the king thought that all the land that stretched before him belonged to the rich and powerful Marquis of Carabas.

At last Puss reached a huge castle. It belonged to the person who owned these lands, a fearsome ogre. Puss knocked at the door and said, "I could not pass the castle of such a fine gentleman without paying my respects."

The ogre, flattered by these words, invited Puss in.

Then Puss said, "I understand that you have magical powers, that you can change yourself into any kind of animal."

"It's true!" the ogre said in a thundering voice. In an instant

he transformed himself into an enormous elephant!

"Fantastic!" cried Puss.

Then the room was filled with a roar and the huge elephant became a fierce lion.

"Amazing!" cried Puss as he nimbly leapt above the lion's reach. "But, it must be easy to turn yourself into something huge. However, it must be impossible to turn into something very, very small — like a mouse — even for you!"

"Impossible? Impossible!" roared the lion. "Hah!"

In a flash the mighty lion became a tiny mouse. That was exactly what Puss had wanted! He sprang and pounced on the mouse…and that was the end of the once giant ogre!

In a short time, the king's carriage arrived at the castle.

Puss stood confidently at the gate and called out, "Welcome to the castle of my master, the Marquis of Carabas!"

The king was amazed. "Is this castle yours, too?" he asked the miller's son. By now the young man understood Puss's plan and nodded modestly. He took the princess's hand, and led her into the castle.

The servants prepared a great feast, for they would much rather obey Puss than the ogre.

The king was so impressed with the young Marquis that he said, "I would be honored to have you marry my daughter."

So the poor miller's son married the princess and became known in all the land as the Marquis of Carabas. He ruled wisely and fairly over the kingdom that had belonged to the ogre. As for Puss, he became a lord of the court and never had to chase mice again — except for fun.

Rapunzel
& The Seven Ravens

Rapunzel

Once there was a poor man and woman who lived in a humble cottage. Next to the cottage was a walled garden filled with wonderful flowers and vegetables. The garden belonged to a woman named Dame Gothel, who was really a witch.

The woman in the little cottage was soon to have her first child. She spent many hours resting by her window, gazing over the wall at the beautiful garden. The first shoots of rapunzel, a delicious leafy plant, were starting to come up. She

watched them longingly and began to crave the rapunzel so much that she refused to eat anything else.

"I shall die unless I have some rapunzel from that garden," she told her husband.

Seeing his wife so pale and hungry, the poor man decided to get her some rapunzel no matter what the risk. That night he climbed over the garden wall and stole a handful of rapunzel.

His wife made a salad and ate it hungrily. But it tasted so good, so very good, that her craving became even greater.

Because he loved her, the husband wanted to get more rapunzel for his wife. So the next night he climbed over the wall again. But this time, as he

landed in the garden, a stern voice startled him. There stood the witch.

"How dare you steal my rapunzel!" she said. "You shall pay dearly for this!"

"Oh, please," said the terrified man. "I did it for my wife who will soon bear our child. She felt such a craving that she thought she would die."

"Very well," said the witch, "If that is so, you may have the rapunzel, but I must have something in return."

"Anything!" cried the man.

"I will take your child," said the witch. "The child will have a good life, for I shall care for it tenderly like a mother."

The man did not want to agree, but when Dame Gothel

fixed him with her magic witch's stare, he could not refuse.

When the child was born, the witch came and took the baby away. She named her Rapunzel after the delicious plant that her mother had craved so much.

The years went by, and Rapunzel grew to be the most beautiful child in the land. Dame Gothel did treat her kindly, but when Rapunzel was twelve years old, the witch took her deep into the forest. She shut her in a tower that had no door and only a single window at the very top. When the witch wished to visit her, she would stand beneath the window and call up to her:

Rapunzel, Rapunzel,
Let down your hair.

Rapunzel had long hair as beautiful as spun gold. Each time she heard the witch's voice, Rapunzel would undo her braids and fasten them to the window latch. They fell all the way to the

ground. Then the witch would climb up into the tower, using Rapunzel's hair.

Time went by slowly for Rapunzel, alone in the tower. Often she sang to pass the hours. She had a lovely voice that filled the forest with music.

One day, when Rapunzel was nearly grown, a prince rode through the forest and heard her singing. Touched by the loveliness of her voice, he longed to see her, but he could find no door to the tower. Tying his horse to a tree, he hid in the bushes hoping for Rapunzel to appear. Then the witch came to the tower and he heard her call:

Rapunzel, Rapunzel,
Let down your hair.

Immediately he saw Rapunzel let down her braids, and the witch climbed up to her.

"If that is the only way to reach the girl with the beautiful voice, then I will try it," the prince thought.

So at dark, he went to the tower and called:

Rapunzel, Rapunzel,
Let down your hair.

When Rapunzel's hair came down, the prince climbed up.

"Who are you?" Rapunzel cried in fright, for she had never

seen a man before. But the prince spoke gently and told her how he had been so moved by her singing and longed to see her. Rapunzel was glad to have a friend and so the prince visited her often. They grew to love one another very much.

One day the prince said, "Rapunzel, please be my wife and come with me."

"Yes!" Rapunzel replied, "but how will escape from the tower?" Just then she thought of a plan. "Each time you come to visit me, bring a small piece

of silk. I will tie them together to make a ladder and climb down," she said.

The prince did as she asked, and the witch noticed nothing. But one day, in a moment of forgetfulness, Rapunzel said to the witch, "Why are you so much heavier to bring up than the prince?"

"Wicked girl!" Dame Gothel cried. "I shut you away from the world and you have deceived me!"

In a rage, the witch grabbed a pair of scissors and cut off Rapunzel's beautiful hair. Poor Rapunzel wept bitterly, but the heartless witch was full of anger.

She took Rapunzel to a far-off desert separated from the forest by miles of sand. She left her there to live in misery.

Then the witch returned to the tower, attached Rapunzel's severed braids to the window latch and waited. That evening, the prince came to the tower and called softly:

Rapunzel, Rapunzel,
Let down your hair.

The witch let down Rapunzel's hair and hid while the prince climbed through the window.

Instead of his dearest Rapunzel, the prince was met by the angry witch.

"Your little singing bird is gone!" she cried. "Now only her cat awaits you! You shall never see Rapunzel again!"

The prince was beside himself with grief, and in his sorrow, he threw himself from the tower window. The fall did not kill him, but the thorns he landed on scratched his eyes so that he was blind.

For a long time, the sorrowful prince roamed throughout the world. At last he came to the desert where he heard Rapunzel singing ever so faintly. He followed the sound until he found her, and they embraced joyfully. Rapunzel wept for his blindness, and her tears dropped on his eyes, magically healing them.

They returned to the prince's kingdom where they soon were married. In time they became the parents of twins, a boy and a girl, each with beautiful golden hair like their mother's. Together they lived happily for many years to come.

The Seven Ravens

There once was a man who had seven sons but no daughter. Soon his wife had another child, and—at last—it was a girl. The man was overjoyed, yet the child was so weak and frail that she had to be baptized at once. Quickly, the father sent one of his sons to the well for water. The other six soon followed. Each one wanted to draw the water for the baptism of their new sister, but as they quarreled over the water pitcher, it fell into the well. Frightened, they didn't dare go home.

The father grew impatient waiting for his sons. Angry and afraid the baby girl might die unbaptized, he cried out, "I wish they all would turn into ravens!"

No sooner were the words spoken than he looked up and saw seven coal-black ravens flying overhead.

"Oh, no! What have I done?" he said. But the poor man could not undo the curse.

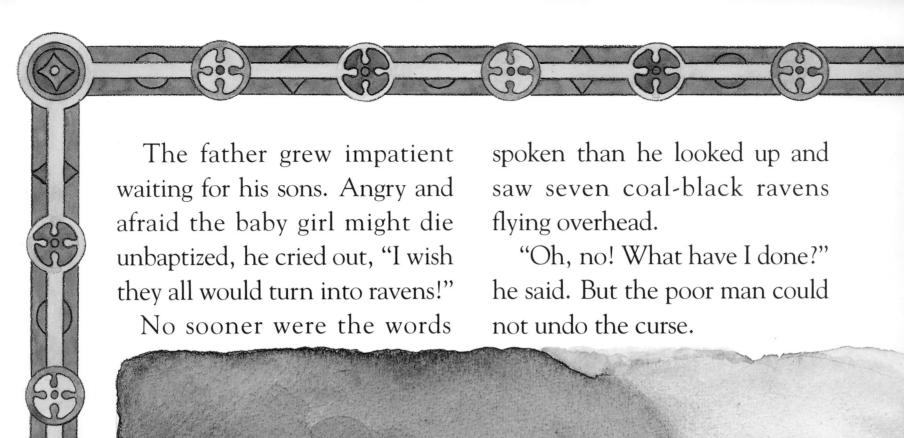

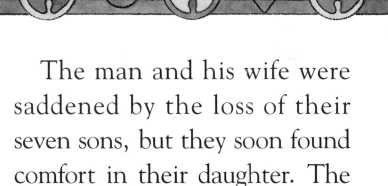

The man and his wife were saddened by the loss of their seven sons, but they soon found comfort in their daughter. The pretty girl grew stronger and more beautiful every day. For a long time the girl did not even know her brothers existed. But one day, she overheard someone talking. The person said that she was the one to blame for the misfortune of her brothers.

These words made her very unhappy. The girl went to her father and mother and asked if she ever had any brothers and, if so, what had become of them. Her parents could no longer keep their secret. Her brothers' tragedy had been an act of fate, they said, and she was not to blame.

But from that time on, the girl's conscience tormented her. She felt she had to do whatever she could to find her brothers, so one day, she went out into the world in hope of finding them. All she took with her was a ring that belonged to her parents to remember them by, a jug of water, a loaf of bread, and a little stool to sit upon when she was tired and needed to rest.

The girl traveled on and on, farther and farther, until she reached the end of the world. She journeyed to the Sun, but it was much too hot to approach and she thirstily drank her water. She ran quickly away. She went to the Moon, but it was too cold and gave her an awful chill. Shivering and hungry, she ate her bread.

So she kept traveling until she came to the Stars, who were cheerful and kind. The Morning Star gave her a tiny key and said, "With this key you can enter the Glass Mountain, the place where you will find your brothers."

The girl took the key and carefully wrapped it in a cloth. She traveled on until she came

to the Glass Mountain, where the entrance gate was indeed locked. The girl took out her cloth and unfolded it—but the tiny key was gone!

What was she to do? Determined to save her brothers, the good sister reached out her slender little finger and bravely put it into the big lock. The gate opened! Just then a dwarf approached her and said, "What are you looking for?"

"My brothers, the seven ravens," she replied.

"My seven lords, the ravens, are not at home," he answered. "But if you wait, they will return soon."

Then the dwarf set the table with the ravens' seven little dishes and seven little cups. The

girl was so hungry that she ate a morsel from every plate and had a sip from every cup. Suddenly, with a whirring of wings, the ravens arrived. Running to hide, the girl dropped the ring she had brought with her in the last cup.

The ravens went straight to their dinners. Each one said, "Who has eaten from my plate and drunk from my cup? It is a human mouth!"

When the seventh raven got to the bottom of his cup, the ring tumbled out. He realized it was his parents' ring and said, "If only our sister might be here. At last we would be free of the spell."

The girl, who was hiding behind a door, heard his wish and stepped out. Immediately, the ravens took on their human form. There stood her seven brothers! They hugged and kissed and happily returned home.